MONSTER HOUSE™

TROUBLE ON OAK STREET

by Bobbi JG Weiss and David Cody Weiss

Ready-to-Read

Simon Spotlight
New York   London   Toronto   Sydney

SIMON SPOTLIGHT

An imprint of Simon & Schuster
Children's Publishing Division
1230 Avenue of the Americas, New York, New York 10020
© 2006 by Columbia Pictures Industries, Inc.
All Rights Reserved.

SIMON SPOTLIGHT, READY-TO-READ, and colophon are
registered trademarks of Simon & Schuster, Inc.
Manufactured in the United States of America
First Edition
2 4 6 8 10 9 7 5 3 1
CIP data for this book is available from the Library of Congress.
ISBN-13: 978-1-4169-1822-6
ISBN-10: 1-4169-1822-1

DJ Walters watched the house across
the street. He knew it was haunted.
It scared kids and ate toys!
"What will it do tomorrow
on Halloween?" he wondered.

When he told his friend Chowder

about the house, Chowder did not

seem to care.

He wanted to go trick-or-treating.

"I am not going," DJ told him.

"We are too grown up for that."

The boys decided to play ball.

When Chowder missed a basket,

his ball rolled across the street.

It stopped on the front lawn of the

haunted house—and the house **ate** it!

The boys could not believe
their eyes.
They watched the house all night,
but it didn't do anything else.

But DJ was not fooled.

"There is something evil

going on in there," he said.

"And I need to find out what it is."

The next morning DJ and Chowder
watched as Jenny Bennett headed
toward the Monster House.
She was selling Halloween candy.

DJ and Chowder ran to stop her.

"Do not go any further!" DJ shouted.

"Come here!"

But it was too late.

The house attacked!
It opened its mouth and
pulled Jenny's wagon in.
Wooden teeth chomped down,
but DJ and Chowder saved
Jenny just in time.

"Do you realize what is going

to happen tonight?" DJ asked.

"Hundreds of kids . . . ," said Chowder,

"walking right up to that door . . ."

"I think it's time to call

the police," Jenny said.

Then Officer Landers
and Officer Lister arrived.

"We need your help," Jenny said.

"This house just tried to eat me."

But the police didn't believe them.

"Do not let me catch you near this house again," Officer Landers said. The three kids knew that they would have to save the trick-or-treaters from the Monster House themselves. But how?

It was time to go to an expert.

So DJ and Chowder took Jenny

to the Pizza Freek to meet Skull—

the smartest guy they knew.

"Defeating the beast is simple,"
Skull told them wisely.
"Thou must strike the source
of life—the heart."

The three kids realized that
the heart of the Monster House
was its furnace.

"We have to get inside," Jenny said.

Then DJ got an idea.

They built a dummy and

filled it with cold medicine.

"House eats the medicine," DJ said.

"House goes to sleep. We get in,

douse the fire in the furnace,

and get out!"

Before they could get the dummy to
the front door of the house, Officer
Landers and Officer Lister arrived.
They put DJ, Chowder, and Jenny
into their police car.

Just then the house came to life!

"It's going to eat us!" Chowder cried.

The house chomped down on the
squad car, breaking it in half.
The kids escaped from the car.
When the house was not looking,
the kids ran inside.

There they were, face-to-face

with the inner workings

of the Monster House.

The kids began to search the house

for its source of life: its heart.

But before they could find it,

the house began to shake with anger.

It wanted them out. Jenny quickly

grabbed onto the house's throat

and it spit them out onto the lawn.

The kids watched in awe as the Monster House pulled itself out of the ground and started to walk.

"Ooh, that's new," Chowder said.

Then the house began to chase them!

On the way the Monster House spied
some trick-or-treaters and started
to go after them instead.

"No!" Jenny cried.

They had to save those children.

"Hey, house!" Jenny and

Chowder shouted.

"Over here!"

Then the Monster House
began to chase Chowder!
Chowder led it to a
construction site.

DJ found some dynamite at the site.

Then he turned to Jenny.

"I have a plan," DJ said.

"What is it?" Jenny asked eagerly.

"We have to climb to the top of
    that big crane."

DJ and Jenny started to climb up
the crane. While they climbed, DJ
set the second part of the plan
in motion. "Chowder!" he yelled.

Chowder was driving a
backhoe, trying to distract the
Monster House.

"Can you get the house under
this crane?" DJ asked.

"Piece of cake," Chowder answered.

DJ and Jenny kept climbing the crane.
At the top of the crane, DJ lit
the fuse and turned to face Jenny.
"When I say 'now,' throw me this."
"Okay," she answered. "You can
do this," she said, smiling.

DJ stepped out onto the arm of
the crane, directly above the house.
"NOW!" he yelled. Jenny tossed him
the dynamite and he caught it.
Then he aimed it at the house.
The stick fell down into the chimney,
and the Monster House exploded!

DJ, Chowder, and Jenny
had saved Halloween!
"I think we've earned
some candy," said Jenny.
So the three friends went
trick-or-treating after all.